LOOK AND SAY WITH...
BOBBY THE BUNNY

Story and illustrations
by Michel Rainaud

DERRYDALE BOOKS
New York

Summer is finally here! The (sun) is shining and it's a beautiful day. But Bobby the Bunny has a cold and must stay in (bed). His friend the (squirrel) brings him a big (bottle) of medicine and tells Bobby what he must do to get better. In the morning, Bobby must take one (spoon) of the medicine. For lunch, he must eat a (plate) of (carrots), and for dinner he

must have a fresh head of  .

In a few days, Bobby the  is

better and is ready to leave for his

 in the country.

Bobby is happy to be on his way to the country and he skips through the fields. He rolls around in the grass and sniffs the 🌸🌼. He chases the 🐝 and the 🦋. The sky is blue and ☁️☁️ drift over the tops of the 🌲🌲🌲🌲. Bobby the

 feels so good that he jumps

over a  .

Bobby the  hops into the forest. He spots the cozy of his old friend the under a . The porcupine is sleeping and Bobby is careful not to wake him. As Bobby hops beneath a , he is hit on the head by some ,

 , and   . "Hey, watch out up there!" he shouts. But Bobby smiles when he sees that it's only his friend the  who is cleaning out his house.

It's a long way to his summer house and Bobby the  is soon tired. He lies down to rest in a field full of tall of wheat, bright red , blue , and beautiful . In the field, a is gathering of wheat for the winter. Little are building a new anthill and carry their to their new home. A sits in the warm . What a perfect day to be in the country!

But all of a sudden, the 🐭 runs away, the 🐦 flies off, and the 🐦 sounds a warning. The clever 🦊 must be nearby. Bobby the 🐰 quickly hides behind a

and then jumps into a
full of hay. The sniffs
here and there, and leaves as
quickly as he came.

Everyone is safe again! Bobby the  continues on his journey and finally arrives at his summer .

The first thing he does is open all the  and  to let the fresh air in.

Bobby sits by the window and watches the 🐝🐝 buzz among the pink 🌷🌷🌷 and the 🌸🌸🌸. A 🐞 crawls on a blade of grass, and a 🐛 chews on some green 🍃🍃 so that one day he can become a beautiful 🦋.The 🐦🐦🐦 sing a song to welcome Bobby the 🐰.

There is a nearby with a garden surrounded by a . Bobby takes his basket and picks some pink , red , and wonderful green . Bobby the says hello to a who is busy eating some . The is having a nice red for lunch.

Bobby the  wishes he could take a nap in the garden, but he has a lot to do!

Bobby the  decides to clean his house first. But as he starts, he sees that everything in his 🏠 is already so clean that it shines—even the 🪑🪑!

A 🏺 filled with 🌸 is sitting on the mantel and there is a 🫗 of water on the 🗄️ . A 🧺 filled with food is on the 🟦 and Bobby the 🐰 sits down at the 🟦 to eat this delicious lunch. As he eats, he wonders who has done all this for him. He doesn't see his friend the 🐭 right outside his 🪟 . It was he who came to clean Bobby's 🏠 .

Bobby the has a wonderful summer in the country. But soon the sky is covered by big dark . The announces that summer is over and autumn is here.

The on the trees turn yellow and fall to the ground. They even color the big red that grows at the foot of the . Soon Bobby

the  and his friends
the will have to go back to
their winter homes.

The  sets early behind the  of the church. Bobby knows it is time to return to his  for the winter. But when the winter is over, summer will be on its way once again!